To my loved ones.
You mean the world to me.
—Kirsten

For Gregg, my favorite cookie.
—Carin

Text copyright © 2009 by Kirsten Bramsen
Illustrations copyright © 2009 by Carin Bramsen
Jacket art copyright © 2009 by Carin Bramsen

Visit us on the Web! www.randomhouse.com/kids

Educators and librarians, for a variety of teaching tools, visit us at
www.randomhouse.com/teachers

Library of Congress Cataloging-in-Publication Data
Bramsen, Kirsten.
The yellow tutu / by Kirsten Bramsen ; illustrated by Carin Bramsen. — 1st ed.
p. cm.
Summary: When Margo gets a sunny yellow tutu for her birthday, it is exactly
what she wants, and she wears it to school—on her head.
ISBN 978-0-375-85168-1 (trade)—ISBN 978-0-375-95168-8 (lib. bdg.)—
ISBN 978-0-375-84393-8 (board bk.)
[1. Tutus (Ballet skirts)—Fiction. 2. Individuality—Fiction.]
I. Bramsen, Carin, ill.
II. Title. PZ7.B73576Ye 2009 [E]—dc22 2007012714

MANUFACTURED IN CHINA 10 9 8 7 6 5 4 3 2 1 First Edition

The Yellow Tutu

text by Kirsten Bramsen • illustrated by Carin Bramsen

Random House 🏠 New York

Today was a special day. It was Margo's birthday. She awoke to find a big present at the end of her bed. What could it be?

Was it a doll with long, shiny hair? Was it a rock polisher? Was it an ant farm or a fairy doll with sparkly wings? She stared at the brightly wrapped present for a whole two minutes. Then, unable to wait a second longer, she tore it open.

She couldn't believe her eyes. Inside was the most beautiful thing she had ever seen. It was her dream!

It was . . .

A YELLOW TUTU!!!!

She immediately put it on over her pajamas
and began dancing around her bedroom.

"I'm a princess, la la la la! I am sunshine!"

Margo began to sing,

"I am my sunshine, my only sunshine.
I make me happeeeeeee when skies are gray. . . ."

And then she had an idea. A bright, glittery idea. *If I want to look like sunshine, I'll have to wear my tutu on my head.* So she put her tutu on her head and wore it like a hat.

"Tra
la la
la la!"

Today might be Margo's birthday but it was still a school day. "I'll wear my tutu to school so everyone can see it!" she said.

So she walked to school with her tutu on her head.
She wondered if she would make the flowers grow
because she looked just like the sun.

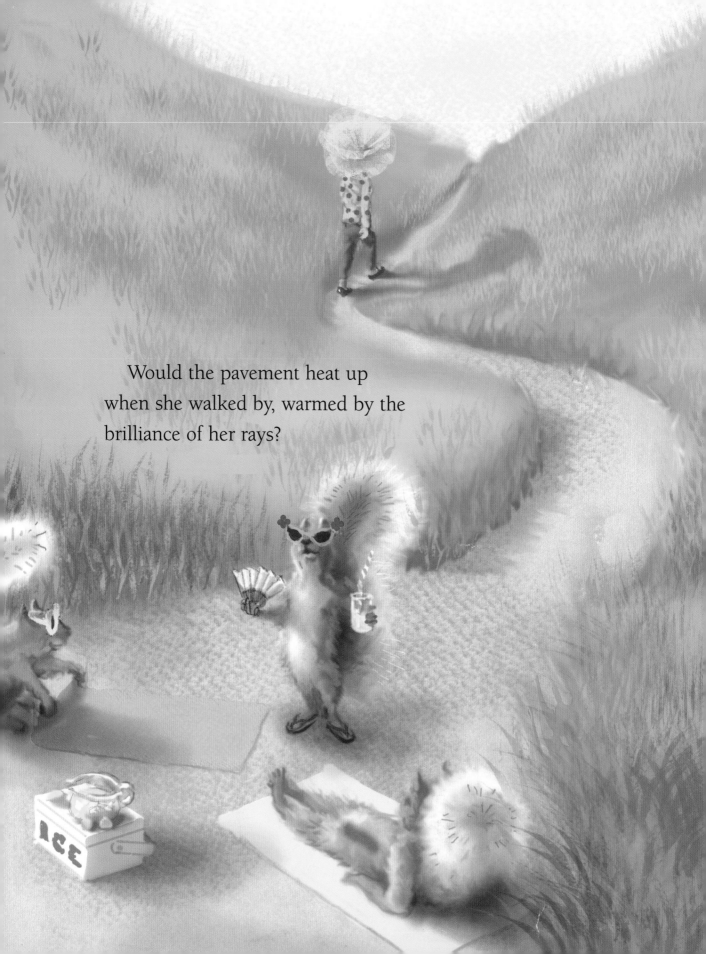

Would the pavement heat up
when she walked by, warmed by the
brilliance of her rays?

Would the grass grow taller and greener?

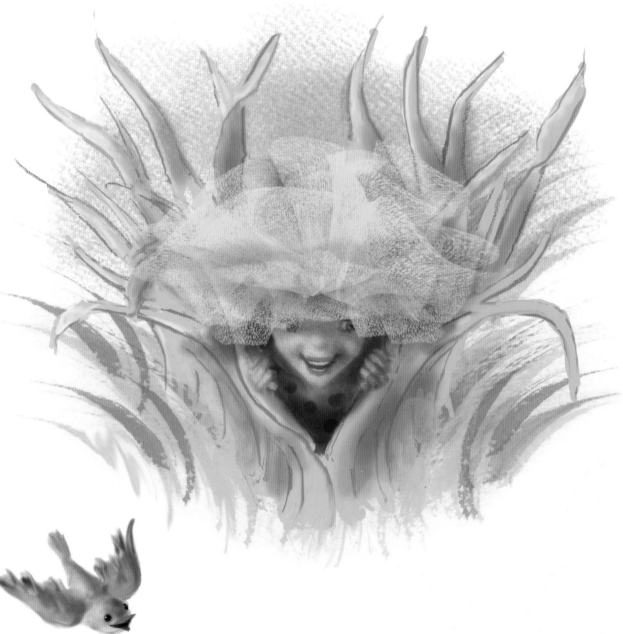

Would the birds sing happily and the bees buzz even louder?

And what would her friends at school think?
Would they recognize her? Or would they be too
amazed for words?

Would they think she was the actual sun and not look straight at her because they wouldn't want to hurt their eyes?

But that is not what happened at all. The kids at school laughed and laughed when they saw the tutu on her head.

"You look stupid with that thing on your head!" one boy said.

"Get that silly tutu off your head," said one girl.
"TUTU-HEAD!!!" they all teased. Another little
girl even tried to yank it off her head.

Margo was surprised.

What was the matter with everyone?

She knew she looked great, exciting, happy,
bright, and beautiful in her new tutu!

"You're just jealous," Margo said. "I think everyone would want a tutu just like this! It's so beautiful! Pearl has a tutu but hers is pink."

"Yeah," they said, "but Pearl wears hers to dance class and NOT on her head."

That's when Pearl said, "I like Margo's yellow tutu and I think she looks just like a sunflower."

Margo said, "Or a lion!

ROARRRRRRRR!"

Margo and Pearl skipped away from the other kids.
"Margo," Pearl said, "would you like to come over to
my house after school and play tea party in our tutus?"
"Oh yes," said Margo.

So Margo and Pearl played tea
party after school that very afternoon.
Margo proudly wore her yellow tutu
on her head, and Pearl decided to
wear hers on her head too.

They thought they looked just like
yellow and pink roses as they drank
their pretend tea.